Read to Me Daddy

Read to Me Daddy

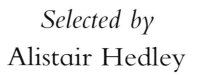

Selected by

Alistair Hedley

Illustrated by

Kate Aldous, Sue Clarke, Claire Henley, Anna Cynthia Leplar,
Jacqueline Mair, Sheila Moxley, Alan Peacock, Karen Perrins,
Scott Rhodes, Jane Tattersfield, and Sara Walker.

This is a Parragon Publishing Book
This edition published in 2002

Parragon Publishing
Queen Street House
4 Queen Street
Bath BA1 1HE, UK

Created by The Albion Press Ltd

ISBN 0-75259-485-0

Printed in China.

CONTENTS

THE STORY OF
THE LITTLE BIRD

Once long ago in a monastery in Ireland there lived a holy
man. He was walking one day in the garden of his monastery,
when he decided to kneel down and pray, to give thanks to
God for the beauty of all the flowers and plants and herbs
around him. As he did so, he heard a small bird singing, and
never before had he heard any song as sweet. When his prayers,
were finished, the monk stood up and listened to the bird, and

when the creature flew away from the garden, singing as it went, he followed it.

In a while they came to a small grove of trees outside the monastery grounds, and there the bird continued its song. As the bird hopped from tree to tree, still singing all the while, the monk carried on following the little creature, until they had gone a great distance. The more the bird sang, the more the monk was enchanted by the music it made.

Eventually, the two had traveled far away from the monastery, and the monk realised that it would soon be nighttime. So reluctantly, he left the bird behind and retraced his steps, arriving back home as the sun was going down in the west. As the sun set, it lit up the sky with all the colors of the rainbow, and the monk thought that the sight was almost as beautiful and heavenly as the song of the little bird he had been listening to all afternoon long.

But the glorious sunset was not the only sight that surprised the monk. As he entered the abbey gates, everything around him seemed changed from before. In the garden grew different plants, in the courtyard the brothers had different faces, and even the abbey buildings seemed to have altered. He knew he was in the right place, yet how could all these changes have taken place in a single afternoon?

The holy man walked across the courtyard and greeted the

first monk he saw. "Brother, how is it that our abbey has changed so much since this morning? There are fresh plants in the garden, new faces amongst the brothers, and even the stones of the church seem different."

The second monk looked at the holy man carefully. "Why do you ask these questions, brother? There have been no changes. Our church and gardens have not altered since morning, and we have no new brothers here—except for yourself, for though you wear the habit of our order, I have not seen you before." And the two monks looked at each other in wonder. Neither could understand what had happened.

When he saw that the

brother was puzzled, the holy man started to tell his story. He told his companion how he had gone to walk in the monastery garden, how he had heard the little bird, and how he had followed the creature far into the countryside to listen to its song.

As the holy man spoke, the expression on the second monk's face turned from puzzlement to surprise. He said, "There is a story in our order about a brother like you who went missing one day after a bird was heard singing. He never returned to the abbey, and no one knew what befell him, and all this happened two hundred years ago."

The holy man looked at his companion and replied, "That is indeed my story. The time of my death has finally arrived. Praised be the Lord for his mercies to me." And the holy man begged the second monk to take his confession and give him absolution, for the hour of his death was near. All this was done, the holy man died before midnight, and he was buried with great solemnity in the abbey church.

Ever since, the monks of the abbey have told this story. They say that the little bird was an angel of the Lord, and that this was God's way of taking the soul of a man who was known for his holiness and his love of the beauties of nature.

SIMPLE GIFTS

'Tis the gift to be simple,
'Tis the gift to be free,
'Tis the gift to come down
Where we ought to be,
And when we find ourselves
In the place just right,
'Twill be in the valley
Of love and delight.
When true simplicity is gained
To bow and to bend
We sha'n't be ashamed,
To turn, turn will be our delight,
Till by turning, turning
We come round right.

ANONYMOUS
AMERICAN, SHAKER SONG

14

LITTLE THINGS

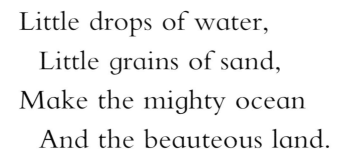

Little drops of water,
　　Little grains of sand,
Make the mighty ocean
　　And the beauteous land.

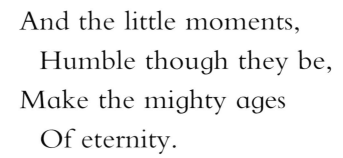

And the little moments,
　　Humble though they be,
Make the mighty ages
　　Of eternity.

So our little errors
　　Lead the soul away,
From the paths of virtue
　　Into sin to stray.

Little deeds of kindness,
　　Little words of love,
Make our earth an Eden,
　　Like the heaven above.

JULIA A. CARNEY

WHOLE DUTY OF CHILDREN

A child should always say what's true,
And speak when he is spoken to,
And behave mannerly at table:
At least as far as he is able.

ROBERT LOUIS STEVENSON

DON'T-CARE

Don't-care didn't care;
  Don't-care was wild.
Don't-care stole plum and pear
  Like any beggar's child.

Don't-care was made to care,
  Don't-care was hung:
Don't-care was put in the pot
  And boiled till he was done.

ANONYMOUS
ENGLISH

THE WIND

Who has seen the wind?
  Neither I nor you;
But when the leaves hang trembling
  The wind is passing through.

Who has seen the wind?
  Neither you nor I;
But when the trees bow down their heads
  The wind is passing by.

CHRISTINA ROSSETTI

18

FROM A RAILWAY CARRIAGE

Faster than fairies, faster than witches,
Bridges and houses, hedges and ditches;
And charging along like troops in a battle,
All through the meadows the horses and cattle:
All of the sights of the hill and the plain
Fly as thick as driving rain;
And ever again, in the wink of an eye,
Painted stations whistle by.

Here is a child who clambers and scrambles,
All by himself and gathering brambles;
Here is a tramp who stands and gazes;
And there is the green for stringing the daisies!
Here is a cart run away in the road
Lumping along with man and load;
And here is a mill, and there is a river:
Each a glimpse and gone for ever!

ROBERT LOUIS STEVENSON

A BABY-SERMON

The lightning and thunder
They go and they come;
But the stars and the stillness
Are always at home.

GEORGE MacDONALD

WAGTAIL AND BABY

A baby watched a ford, whereto
　　A wagtail came for drinking;
A blaring bull went wading through,
　　The wagtail showed no shrinking.

A stallion splashed his way across,
　　The birdie nearly sinking;
He gave his plumes a twitch and toss,
　　And held his own unblinking.

Next saw the baby round the spot
　　A mongrel slowing slinking;
The wagtail gazed, but faltered not
　　In dip and sip and prinking.

A perfect gentleman then neared;
　　The wagtail, in a winking,
With terror rose and disappeared;
　　The baby fell a-thinking.

THOMAS HARDY

21

ROUND AND ROUND
THE GARDEN

Round and round the garden
Like a teddy bear;
One step, two step,
Tickle you under there!

THIS LITTLE PIGGY

This little piggy went to market,
This little piggy stayed at home,
This little piggy had roast beef,
This little piggy had none,
And this little piggy cried, *Wee-wee-wee-wee-wee,*
All the way home.

MY MOTHER AND YOUR MOTHER

My mother and your mother
  Went over the way;
Said my mother to your mother,
  It's chop-a-nose day!

A FACE GAME

Here sits the Lord Mayor;	*Forehead*
Here sit his two men;	*Eyes*
Here sits the cock;	*Right cheek*
Here sits the hen;	*Left cheek*
Here sit the little chickens;	*Tip of nose*
Here they run in,	*Mouth*
Chinchopper, chinchopper,	
Chinchopper, chin!	*Chuck the chin*

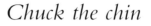

THE FLY

Little Fly,
Thy summer's play
My thoughtless hand
Has brushed away.

Am not I
A fly like thee?
Or art not thou
A man like me?

For I dance,
And drink, and sing,
Till some blind hand
Shall brush my wing.

If thought is life
And strength and breath,
And the want
Of thought is death;

Them am I
A happy fly,
If I live
Or if I die.

WILLIAM BLAKE

26

LADYBIRD! LADYBIRD!

Ladybird! Ladybird! Fly away home,
Night is approaching, and sunset is come:
The herons are flown to their trees by the Hall;
Felt, but unseen, the damp dewdrops fall.
This is the close of a still summer day;
Ladybird! Ladybird! haste! fly away!

EMILY BRONTË

TO MARKET, TO MARKET

To market, to market,
To buy a plum bun;
Home again, come again,
Market is done.

TO MARKET, TO MARKET, TO BUY A FAT PIG

To market, to market, to buy a fat pig,
Home again, home again, dancing a jig;
Ride to the market to buy a fat hog,
Home again, home again, jiggety-jog.

THIS IS THE WAY THE LADIES RIDE

This is the way the ladies ride:
  Tri, tre, tre, tree,
  Tri, tre, tre, tree!
This is the way the ladies ride:
  Tri, tre, tre, tre, tri-tre-tre-tree!

This is the way the gentlemen ride:
  Gallop-a-trot,
  Gallop-a-trot!
This is the way the gentlemen ride:
  Gallop-a-gallop-a-trot!

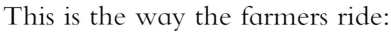

This is the way the farmers ride:
  Hobbledy-hoy,
  Hobbledy-hoy!
This is the way the farmers ride:
  Hobbledy hobbledy-hoy!

LEG OVER LEG

Leg over leg,
　　As the dog went to Dover;
When he came to a stile,
　　Jump he went over.

MICHAEL FINNEGAN

There was an old man called Michael Finnegan
He grew whiskers on his chinnegan
The wind came out and blew them in again
Poor old Michael Finnegan. *Begin again...*

RIDE A COCK-HORSE

Ride a cock-horse to Banbury Cross,
To see a fine lady ride on a white horse,
Rings on her fingers and bells on her toes,
She shall have music wherever she goes.

31

I AM A GOLD LOCK

I am a gold lock.
I am a gold key.
I am a silver lock.
I am a silver key.
I am a brass lock.
I am a brass key.
I am a lead lock.
I am a lead key.
I am a monk lock.
I am a monk key!

I WENT UP ONE PAIR OF STAIRS

FOR TWO VOICES

I went up one pair of stairs.
Just like me.
I went up two pair of stairs.
Just like me.
I went into a room.
Just like me.
I looked out of a window.
Just like me.
And there I saw a monkey.
Just like me.

THE DARK WOOD

In the dark, dark wood, there was
  a dark, dark house,
And in that dark, dark house, there was
  a dark, dark room,
And in that dark, dark room, there was
  a dark, dark cupboard,
And in that dark, dark cupboard, there was
  a dark, dark shelf,
And on that dark, dark shelf, there was
  a dark, dark box,
And in that dark, dark box, there was a
  GHOST!

I MET A MAN

As I was going up the stair
I met a man who wasn't there.
He wasn't there again today—
Oh! how I wish he'd go away!

35

ADAM AND EVE AND PINCHME

Adam and Eve and Pinchme
Went down to the river to bathe.
Adam and Eve were drowned—
Who do you think was saved?

ME, MYSELF, AND I

Me, myself, and I—
We went to the kitchen and ate a pie.
Then my mother she came in
And chased us out with a rolling pin.

PETER PIPER

Peter Piper picked a peck of pickled pepper;
A peck of pickled pepper Peter Piper picked;
If Peter Piper picked a peck of pickled pepper,
Where's the peck of pickled pepper Peter Piper picked?

THE SHORTEST TONGUE TWISTER
Peggy Babcock

THE WELL AT
THE WORLD'S END

There was once a king, a widower, and he had a daughter who was beautiful and good-natured. The king married a queen, who was a widow, and she had a daughter who was as ugly and ill-natured as the king's daughter was fair and good. The queen detested the king's daughter, for no one would notice her own girl while this paragon was beside her, so she made a plan. She sent the king's daughter to the well at the world's end, with a bottle to get some water, thinking she would never come back.

The girl walked far and was beginning to tire when she came upon a pony tethered by the roadside. The pony looked at the girl and spoke: "Ride me, ride me, fair princess."

"Yes, I will ride you," replied the girl, and the pony carried her over a moor covered with prickly gorse and brambles.

Far she rode, and finally she came to the well at the world's end. She took her bottle and lowered it into the well, but the well was too deep and she could not fill the bottle. Then three old men came up to her, saying, "Wash us, wash us, fair maid, and dry us with your linen apron."

So she washed the men and in return they lowered her bottle into the well and filled it with water.

When they had finished, the three men looked at the girl and spoke her future. "If she was fair before, she will be ten times more beautiful," said the first.

"A diamond and a ruby and a pearl shall drop from her mouth every time she speaks," predicted the second.

"Gold and silver shall come from her hair when she combs it," said the third.

The king's daughter returned to court, and to everyone's amazement, these predictions came true.

All were happy with the girl's good fortune, except for the

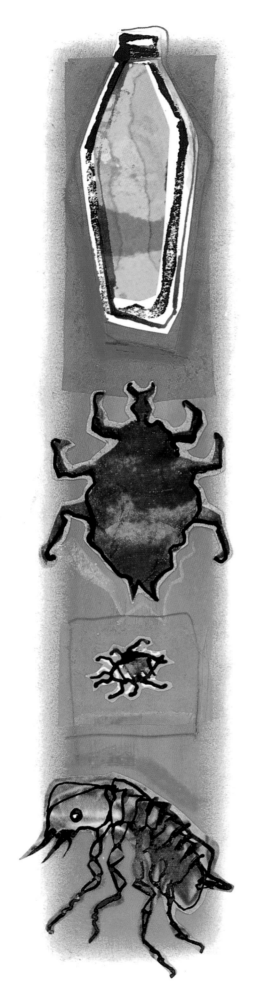

queen and her daughter. The queen decided that she would send her own daughter to the well at the world's end, to get her the same gifts. After travelling far, the girl came to the pony, as the king's daughter had done before her. By now, the beast was tethered once more. But when the creature asked her to ride it, the queen's daughter replied, "Don't you see I am a queen's daughter? I will not ride you, you filthy beast."

The proud girl walked on, and she soon came to the moor covered with gorse and brambles. It was hard going for the girl, and the thorns cut her feet badly. Soon she could hardly walk with the pain.

After a long and painful walk across the moor, the queen's daughter came to the well at the world's end. She lowered her bottle, but like the king's daughter, found that it would not reach the water in the well. Then she heard the three old men speaking: "Wash us, wash us, fair maid, and dry us with your linen apron."

And the proud daughter replied, "You

nasty, filthy creatures, do you think a queen's daughter can be bothered to wash you, and dry your dirty faces with my fine clean clothes?"

So the old men refused to dip the girl's bottle into the well. Instead, they turned to her and began to predict her future: "If she was ugly before, she will be ten times uglier," said the first.

"Each time she speaks, a frog and a toad will jump from her mouth," predicted the second.

"When she combs her hair, lice and fleas will appear," said the third.

With these curses ringing in her ears, the unhappy girl returned home. Her mother was distraught when she saw her daughter, for she was indeed uglier than before, and frogs, toads, fleas, and lice, jumped from her. In the end, she left the king's court, and married a poor cobbler. The king's fair and good-natured daughter married a handsome prince, and was happy—and good-natured—for the rest of her long life.

MY GRANDMOTHER SENT ME

My grandmother sent me a new-fashioned three cornered cambric country cut handkerchief. Not an old-fashioned three cornered cambric country cut handkerchief, but a new-fashioned three cornered cambric country cut handkerchief.

ROBERT ROWLEY

Robert Rowley rolled a round roll round,
A round roll Robert Rowley rolled round;
Where rolled the round roll Robert Rowley
rolled round?

SWAN SWAM OVER THE SEA

Swan swam over the sea—
Swim, swan, swim,
Swan swam back again,
Well swum swan.

HEY, DOROLOT, DOROLOT!

Hey, dorolot, dorolot!
Hey, dorolay, dorolay!
Hey, my bonny boat, bonny boat,
Hey, drag away, drag away!

THERE WAS A MAN AND HIS NAME WAS DOB

There was a man, and his name was Dob,
And he had a wife, and her name was Mob,
And he had a dog, and he called it Cob,
And she had a cat, called Chitterabob.
   Cob, says Dob,
   Chitterabob, says Mob,
   Cob was Dob's dog,
   Chitterabob Mob's cat.

DIBBITY, DIBBITY, DIBBITY, DOE

Dibbity, dibbity, dibbity, doe,
Give me a pancake
 And I'll go.
Dibbity, dibbity, dibbity, ditter,
Please to give me
 A bit of a fritter.

A THORN

I went to the wood and got it;
I sat me down and looked at it;
The more I looked at it the less I liked it;
And I brought it home because I couldn't help it.

TEETH

Thirty white horses upon a red hill,
Now they tramp, now they champ,
now they stand still.

A STAR

I have a little sister, they call her Peep, Peep;
She wades the waters deep, deep, deep;
She climbs the mountains high, high, high;
Poor little creature she has but one eye.

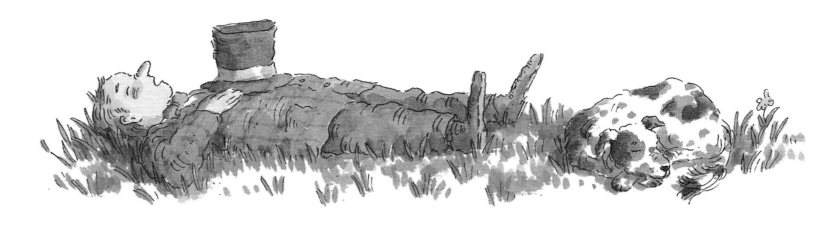

TOMMY TROT

Tommy Trot, a man of law,
Sold his bed and lay upon straw:
Sold the straw and slept on grass,
To buy his wife a looking glass.

TUMBLING

In jumping and tumbling
     We spend the whole day,
Till night by arriving
     Has finished our play.

What then? One and all,
     There's no more to be said,
As we tumbled all day,
     So we tumble to bed.

HUSH, LITTLE BABY

Hush, little baby, don't say a word,
Papa's going to buy you a mocking bird.

If the mocking bird won't sing,
Papa's going to buy you a diamond ring.

If the diamond ring turn to brass,
Papa's going to buy you a looking-glass.

If the looking-glass gets broke,
Papa's going to buy you a billy-goat.

If that billy-goat runs away,
Papa's going to buy you another today.

ANONYMOUS
AMERICAN

THE MOUSE'S LULLABY

Oh, rock–a–by, baby mouse, rock–a–by, so!
When baby's asleep to the baker's I'll go,
And while he's not looking I'll pop from a hole,
And bring to my baby a fresh penny roll.

Palmer Cox

A CRADLE SONG

Golden slumbers kiss your eyes,
Smiles awake you when you rise.
Sleep, pretty wantons, do not cry,
And I will sing a lullaby:
Rock them, rock them, lullaby.

Care is heavy, therefore sleep you;
You are care, and care must keep you.
Sleep, pretty wantons, do not cry,
And I will sing a lullaby:
Rock them, rock them, lullaby.

THOMAS DEKKER

52

A CHILD'S EVENING PRAYER

Ere on my bed my limbs I lay,

God grant me grace my prayers to say:

O God, preserve my mother dear

In strength and health for many a year;

And, O! preserve my father too,

And may I pay him reverence due;

And may I my best thoughts employ

To be my parents' hope and joy;

And O! preserve my brothers both

From evil doings and from sloth,

And may we always love each other

Our friends, out father, and our mother:

And still, O Lord, to me impart

An innocent and grateful heart,

That after my great sleep I may

Awake to thy eternal day! Amen.

SAMUEL TAYLOR COLERIDGE

SONG OF THE SKY LOOM

O our Mother the Earth, O our Father the Sky,

Your children are we, and with tired backs

We bring you the gifts that you love.

Then weave for us a garment of brightness;

May the warp be the white light of morning,

May the weft be the red light of evening,

May the fringes be the falling rain,

May the border be the standing rainbow.

Thus weave for us a garment of brightness,

That we may walk fittingly where birds sing,

That we way walk fittingly where grass is green,

O our Mother the Earth, O our Father the sky.

ANONYMOUS
NATIVE AMERICAN, TEWA

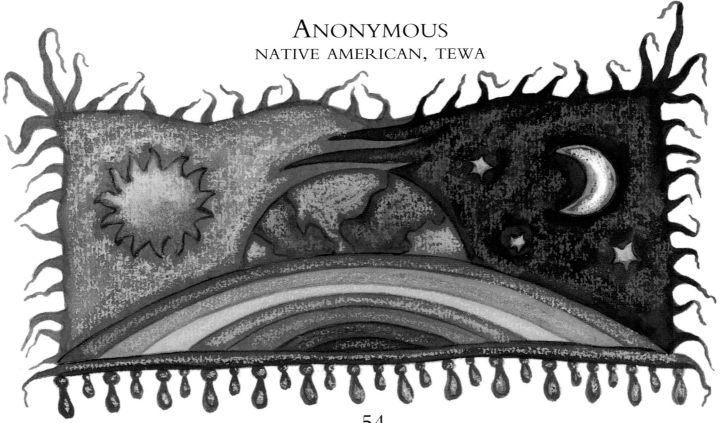

PUTTING THE WORLD TO BED

The little snow people are hurrying down
   From their home in the clouds overhead;
They are working as hard as ever they can,
   Putting the world to bed.

Every tree in a soft fleecy nightgown they clothe;
   Each part has its night-cap of white.
And o'er the cold ground a thick cover they spread
   Before they say good night.

And so they come eagerly sliding down,
   With a swift and silent tread,
Always as busy as busy can be,
   Putting the world to bed.

ESTHER W. BUXTON

55

THE
SPRIGHTLY TAILOR

Long ago, in a castle called Sandell, lived a laird called the great MacDonald. MacDonald liked his comfort, and favored garments called trews, which were a combination of vest and pants in one piece. One day the laird needed some new trews, and called for the local tailor.

When the tailor arrived the great MacDonald told him what he wanted. "I'll pay you extra," promised the laird, "if you will make the trews in the church by night." For MacDonald had heard that the church was haunted by a fearful monster,

and he wanted to see how the tailor fared when faced with this beast.

The tailor had also heard stories about the monster. But he was a sprightly fellow who liked a challenge—especially if it was going to lead to some extra money. So that very night he walked up the glen, through the churchyard gate, and into the dark church. Finding a tombstone where he could sit, he got to work on the trews, and very soon the garment was taking shape.

After a while, the tailor felt the floor of the church begin to shake beneath him. A hole seemed to open up in the stone floor and a large and gruesome head appeared. "Do you see this great head of mine?" a voice boomed.

"I see that, but I'll sew these," replied the tailor, holding up the trews.

The head paused as the tailor was speaking, then began to rise again, revealing a thick, muscular neck. "Do you see this great neck of mine?" the monster asked.

"I see that, but I'll sew these," replied the tailor.

Next the creature's shoulders and trunk came into view. "Do you see this great chest of mine?"

"I see that, but I'll sew these," said the tailor. And he carried on sewing, although, to tell the truth, some of the stitches were a little less neat than normal.

Now the beast was rising quickly, and the tailor could make

out its arms. Its voice echoed in the stone building: "Do you see these great arms of mine?"

"I see those, but I'll sew these," replied the tailor. He gritted his teeth and carried on with his work as before, for he wanted to finish by daybreak and claim his payment from the great MacDonald.

The tailor's needle was flying now, as the monster gave a great grunt and lifted his first leg out of the ground. "Do you see this great leg of mine?" he said, his voice getting even louder.

"I see that, but I'll sew these," replied the tailor, making his final stitches a little longer, so that he could finish his work before the monster could climb out of his hole.

As the creature began to raise its other leg, the tailor blew out his candle, gathered up his things, and bundled the completed trews under one arm. He made for the door as the monster was emerging, and the tailor could hear the creature's footsteps echoing on the stone floor as he ran out into the open air.

Now the tailor could see the glen stretching in front of him, and he ran for his life, faster than he had ever ran before, for all that he was a nimble man. The monster roared at him to stop, but the tailor hurried on, his feet hardly touching the ground, and finally the great MacDonald's castle loomed up ahead of him and the tailor knew he had a chance to reach its gates.

Quickly the gates opened, and quickly they closed behind the tailor—and not a moment too soon, for as the great wooden gates slammed shut, the monster crashed to a halt and struck a resounding blow on the wall to show how frustrated he was at missing his goal when he had got so near.

To this day, the monster's handprint can be seen on the wall of the castle at Sandell. MacDonald paid the sprightly tailor for his work, and gave him a handsome bonus for braving the haunted church. The laird liked his smart new trews, and never realised that some of the stitches were longer and less neat than the others.

NIGHT SOUNDS

Midnight's bell goes ting, ting, ting, ting, ting,

Then dogs do howl, and not a bird does sing

But the nightingale, and she cries twit, twit, twit;

Owls then on every bough do sit;

Ravens croak on chimneys' tops;

The cricket in the chamber hops;

The nibbling mouse is not asleep,

But he goes peep, peep, peep, peep, peep;

   And the cats cry mew, mew, mew,

   And still the cats cry mew, mew, mew.

THOMAS MIDDLETON

SWEET AND LOW

Sweet and low, sweet and low,
    Wind of the western sea,
Low, low, breathe and blow,
    Wind of the western sea!
Over the rolling waters go,
Come from the dying moon, and blow,
    Blow him again to me;
While my little one, while my pretty one, sleeps.

Sleep and rest, sleep and rest,
    Father will come to thee soon;
Rest, rest, on mother's breast,
    Father will come to thee soon;
Father will come to his babe in the nest,
Silver sails all out of the west
    Under the silver moon:
Sleep, my little one, sleep, my pretty one, sleep.

ALFRED, LORD TENNYSON

DREAMS

Beyond, beyond the mountain line,
　　The grey-stone and the boulder,
Beyond the growth of dark green pine,
　　That crowns its western shoulder,
There lies that fairy land of mine,
　　Unseen of a beholder.

Its fruits are all like rubies rare,
　　Its streams are clear as glasses:
There golden castles hang in air,
　　And purple grapes in masses,
And noble knights and ladies fair
　　Come riding down the passes.

Ah me! they say if I could stand
　　Upon those mountain ledges,
I should but see on either hand
　　Plain fields and dusty hedges:
And yet I know my fairy land
　　Lies somewhere o'er their hedges.

CECIL FRANCES ALEXANDER

DREAMS

Here we are all, by day; by night we are hurled
By dreams, each one into a several world.

ROBERT HERRICK

I HAD A LITTLE NUT TREE

I had a little nut tree, nothing would it bear,
But a silver nutmeg, and a golden pear;
The King of Spain's daughter came to visit me,
And all for the sake of my little nut tree.
I skipped over water, I danced over sea,
And all the birds of the air couldn't catch me.

HOW MANY MILES TO BABYLON?

How many miles to Babylon?—
Threescore and ten.
Can I get there by candlelight?—
Aye, and back again!

LADY MOON

Lady Moon, Lady Moon, where are you roving?
    Over the sea.
Lady Moon, Lady Moon, whom are you loving?
    All that love me.

Are you not tired with rolling, and never
    Resting to sleep?
Why look so pale, and so sad, as for ever
    Wishing to weep?

Ask me not this, little child, if you love me;
    You are too bold;
I must obey my dear Father above me,
    And do as I'm told.

Lady Moon, Lady Moon, where are you roving?
    Over the sea.
Lady Moon, Lady Moon, whom are you loving?
    All that love me.

RICHARD MONCKTON MILNES, LORD HOUGHTON

66

THE MOON

The moon has a face like the clock in the hall;
She shines on thieves on the garden wall,
On streets and fields and harbour quays,
And birdies asleep in the forks of the trees.

The squalling cat and the squeaking mouse,
The howling dog by the door of the house,
The bat that lies in bed at noon,
All love to be out by the light of the moon.

But all of the things that belong to the day
Cuddle to sleep to be out of her way;
And flowers and children close their eyes
Till up in the morning the sun shall arise.

ROBERT LOUIS STEVENSON

FROG WENT A-COURTIN'

Mr Froggie went a-courtin' an' he did ride;
Sword and pistol by his side.

He went to Missus Mousie's hall,
Gave a loud knock and gave a loud call.

"Pray, Missus Mousie, air you within?"
"Yes, kind sir, I set an' spin."

He tuk Miss Mousie on his knee,
An' sez, "Miss Mousie, will ya marry me?"

Miss Mousie blushed an' hung her head,
"You'll have t'ask Uncle Rat," she said.

"Not without Uncle Rat's consent
Would I marry the Pres-i-dent."

Uncle Rat jumped up an' shuck his fat side,
To think his niece would be Bill Frog's bride.

Nex' day Uncle Rat went to town,
To git his niece a weddin' gown.

Whar shall the weddin' supper be?
'Way down yander in a holler tree.

First come in was a Bumble-bee,
Who danced a jig with Captain Flea.

Next come in was a Butterfly,
Sellin' butter very high.

An' when they all set down to sup,
A big gray goose come an' gobbled 'em all up.

An' this is the end of one, two, three,
The Rat an' the Mouse an' the little Froggie.

ANONYMOUS
AMERICAN

THE DUEL

The gingham dog and the calico cat
Side by side on the table sat;
'Twas half-past twelve, and (what do you think!)
Nor one nor t'other had slept a wink!
The old Dutch clock and the Chinese plate
Appeared to know as sure as fate
There was going to be a terrible spat.
(I wasn't there; I simply state
What was told to me by the Chinese plate!)

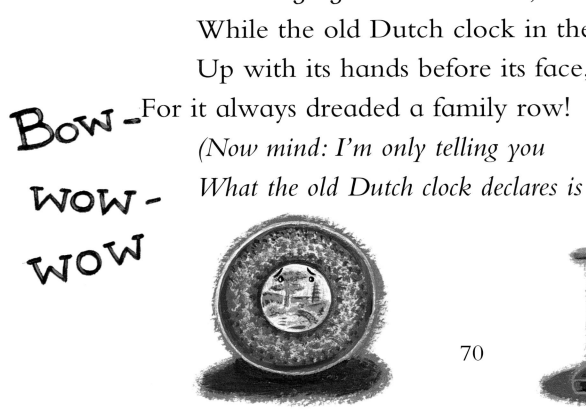

The gingham dog went "Bow-wow-wow!
And the calico cat replied "mee-ow!"
The air was littered, an hour or so,
With bits of gingham and calico,
While the old Dutch clock in the chimney-place
Up with its hands before its face,
For it always dreaded a family row!
(Now mind: I'm only telling you
What the old Dutch clock declares is true!)

Mee-ow

Bow-
wow-
wow

The Chinese plate looked very blue,
And wailed, "Oh, dear! what shall we do?"
But the gingham dog and the calico cat
Wallowed this way and tumbled that,
    Employing every tooth and claw
    In the awfullest way you ever saw—
And, oh! how the gingham and calico flew!
    (Don't fancy I exaggerate!
    I got my news from the Chinese plate!)

Next morning, where the two had sat,
They found no trace of dog or cat;
And some folks think unto this day
That burglars stole that pair away!
    But the truth about the cat and pup
    Is this: they ate each other up!
Now what do you really think of that!
    (The old Dutch clock it told me so,
    And that is how I came to know.)

EUGENE FIELD

ELDORADO

Gaily bedight
A gallant knight,
In sunshine and in shadow,
Had journeyed long,
Singing a song,
In search of Eldorado.

But he grew old—
This knight so bold—
And o'er his heart a shadow
Fell as he found
No spot of ground
That looked like Eldorado.

And, as his strength
Failed him at length,
He met a pilgrim shadow:
"Shadow," said he,
"Where can it be,
This land of Eldorado?"

"Over the mountains
Of the Moon,
Down the valley of the Shadow,
Ride, boldly ride,"
The shade replied,
"If you seek for Eldorado."

EDGAR ALLAN POE

THE WAR SONG OF DINAS VAWR

The mountain sheep are sweeter,
But the valley sheep are fatter;
We therefore deemed it meeter
To carry off the latter.
We made an expedition;
We met a host and quelled it;
We forced a strong position,
And killed the men who held it.

On Dyfed's richest valley.
Where herds of kine were browsing,
We made a mighty sally,
To furnish our carousing.
Fierce warriors rushed to meet us;
We met them and o'erthrew them:
They struggled hard to beat us;
But we conquered them, and slew them.

As we drove out prize at leisure,
The king marched forth to catch us;
His rage surpassed all measure,
But his people could not match us.
He fled to his hall pillars;

And, ere our force we led off,
Some sacked his house and cellars,
While others cut his head off.

We there, in strife bewildering,
Spilt blood enough to swim in:
We orphaned many children,
And widowed many women.
The eagles and the ravens
We glutted with our foemen:
The heroes and the cravens,
The spearmen and the bowmen.

We brought away from battle,
And much their land bemoaned them,
Two thousand head of cattle,
And the head of him who owned them:
Edynfed, King of Dyfed,
His head was borne before us;
His wine and beasts supplied our feasts,
And his overthrow, our chorus,

THOMAS LOVE PEACOCK

THE
CRY OF VENGEANCE

Long ago in the ancient town of Bala lived a wicked prince called Tegid Foel. All his people feared him, for if anyone got in his way, or disagreed with him, the prince had them killed.

Some men plotted to dethrone the prince, but none of them succeeded, for Tegid Foel surrounded himself with guards and henchmen who were almost as ruthless as himself. One day, the prince heard a small voice, whispering in his ear, "Vengeance will come, vengeance will come!" Tegid took no

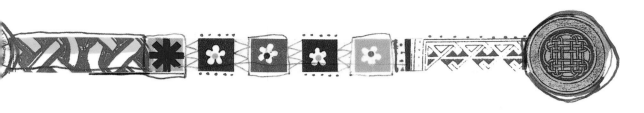

notice of the voice, even though he heard it again, and soon he heard it every day. And the prince's rule carried on for many years of cruelty, until his three sons were grown up and his first son was married.

Tegid Foel's castle was usually a quiet, sombre place, but one day there was noise of rejoicing there. The wife of Tegid's first son had given birth to her first child, a grandson for the prince, and a great feast was ordered. Everyone in the kingdom was invited—and woe betide anyone who did not attend.

One of those who did not want to come was a young, peace-loving harper from the hills near Bala. He was known as the best musician for miles around, and Tegid wanted him to play at his feast. The harper knew that there would be trouble if he did not go, so he took his harp and strode to the castle.

When the harper arrived, the banquet was already beginning, so he took his place as quickly as he could and began to tune his instrument. When the prince saw him, he roared "Waste no time! Play, harper!" in a voice that sent a chill through all who heard. So the harper sang and played, to the delight of everyone in the hall. It seemed as if his music had brought some tranquillity and beauty to the place, where the atmosphere was usually brooding and evil.

At around midnight, there was an interval, and the harper strolled outside in the courtyard to relax for a while. As he did so, a voice whispered in his ear, "Vengeance has come, vengeance has come." Then he saw a small bird that seemed to be beckoning to him with its beak. The creature seemed to  be telling him to leave the castle.

At first, the harper was doubtful, and he wondered what would become of him if he left the banquet now. But he had always listened to the sounds of nature, so he decided to obey the call, slipping through the castle gates and making for the hills. When he had walked for a while, the harper paused. He realized in horror that he had left his harp behind him in the hall. At once he was in turmoil. His harp was his livelihood. But the guards had probably already noticed that he had gone. If he returned—either to play or to take the harp—he risked losing his head. So he decided to continue on his way.

Far the harper climbed into the hills, leaving the sounds of reveling behind him, until he began to tire and could walk no more. He felt that he was far enough away to be out of reach of the castle guards, who were anyway too intent on reveling to chase him tonight. So he lay down and fell asleep.

At dawn, the harper awoke and stretched and rubbed his eyes. As he looked down to the valley he saw an astounding sight. The town and castle of Bala were no more. In their place was a gigantic lake. The only sign of the previous night's feast was his harp, floating unharmed. As the ripples of the water brought the instrument back to him, the harper sighed with relief that he had listened to the quiet, sweet voice of the bird instead of the harsh, ugly voice of the prince's command.

THERE'S A HOLE IN THE MIDDLE OF THE SEA

There's a hole, there's a hole,
  there's a hole in the middle of the sea.

There's a log in the hole in the middle of the sea.

There's a hole, there's a hole,
  there's a hole in the middle of the sea.

There's a bump on the log in the
  hole in the middle of the sea.

There's a hole, there's a hole,
  there's a hole in the middle of the sea.

There's a frog on the bump on the log
  in the hole in the middle of the sea.

There's a hole, there's a hole,
  there's a hole in the middle of the sea.

There's a fly on the frog on the bump
  on the log in the hole in the middle of the sea.

There's a hole, there's a hole,
  there's a hole in the middle of the sea.

There's a wing on the fly on the frog on the
  bump on the log in the hole in the middle of the sea.

There's a hole, there's a hole,
  there's a hole in the middle of the sea.

There's a flea on the wing on the fly
  on the frog on the bump on the log in the
  hole in the middle of the sea.

There's a hole, there's a hole,
  there's a hole in the middle of the sea.

Anonymous
AMERICAN

THERE WAS AN OLD WOMAN
WHO LIVED IN A SHOE

There was an old woman who lived in a shoe,
She had so many children she didn't know
  what to do;
She gave them some broth without any bread;
And scolded them soundly and put them to bed.

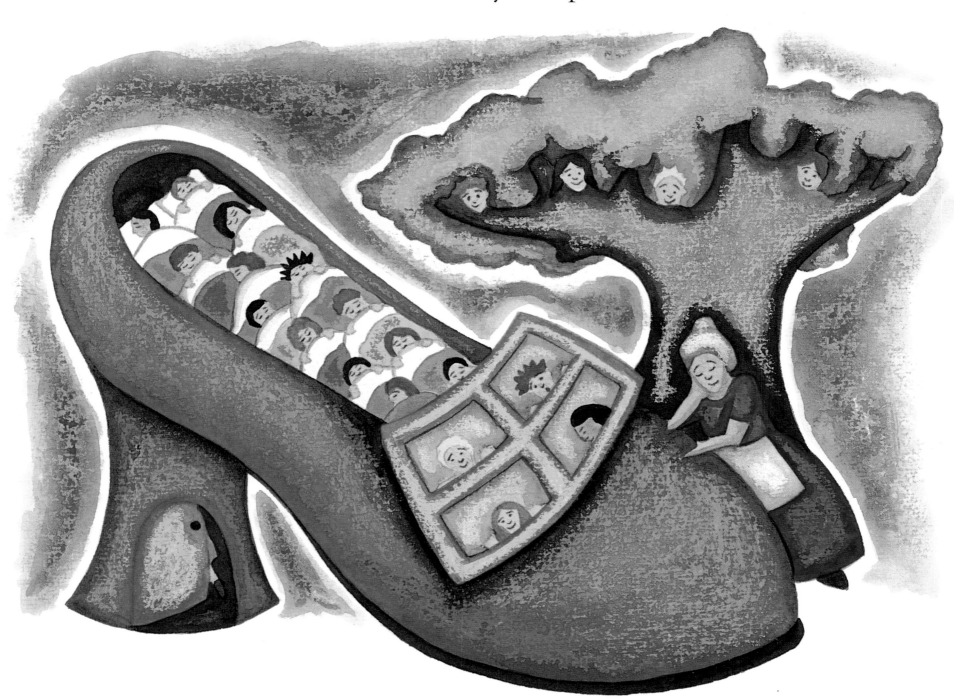

THERE WAS AN OLD WOMAN
AND WHAT DO YOU THINK?

There was an old woman, and what do you think?
She lived upon nothing but victuals and drink:
Victuals and drink were the chief of her diet;
This tiresome old woman could never be quiet.

THERE WAS AN OLD WOMAN
CALLED NOTHING-AT-ALL

There was an old woman called Nothing-at-all,
Who rejoiced in a dwelling exceedingly small;
A man stretched his mouth to its utmost extent,
And down at one gulp house and old woman went.

THERE WAS AN OLD WOMAN
LIVED UNDER A HILL

There was old woman
Lived under a hill,
And if she's not gone
She lives there still.

THERE WAS AN OLD WOMAN
HAD THREE SONS

There was an old woman had three sons,
Jerry, and James, and John:
Jerry was hung, James was drowned,
John was lost and never was found,
And there was an end of the three sons,
Jerry, and James, and John!

THERE WAS AN OLD WOMAN
WENT UP IN A BASKET

There was an old woman went up in a basket,
Seventy times as high as the moon;
What she did there I could not but ask it,
For in her hand she carried a broom.
"Old woman, old woman, old woman," said I,
"Whither oh whither oh whither so high?"
"To sweep the cobwebs from the sky,
And I shall be back again by and by."

OLD BETTY BLUE

Old Betty Blue
　Lost a holiday shoe,
What can old Betty do?
　Give her another
　To match the other,
And then she may swagger in two.

OLD MOTHER GOOSE

Old Mother Goose, when
She wanted to wander,
Would ride through the air
On a very fine gander.

ONE MISTY MOISTY MORNING

One misty moisty morning,
When cloudy was the weather,
There I met an old man
Clothed all in leather;

Clothed all in leather,
With cap under his chin—
How do you do, and how do you do,
And how do you do again!

THERE WAS A CROOKED MAN

There was a crooked man, and he went a
  crooked mile,
He found a crooked sixpence against a
  crooked stile;
He bought a crooked cat, which caught a
  crooked mouse,
And they all lived together in a little crooked house.

AS I WALKED BY MYSELF

As I walked by myself,
And talked to myself,
  Myself said unto me,
Look to thyself,
Take care of thyself,
  For nobody cares for thee.

I answered myself,
And said to myself,
  In the selfsame repartee,
Look to thyself,
Or not look to thyself,
  The selfsame thing will be.

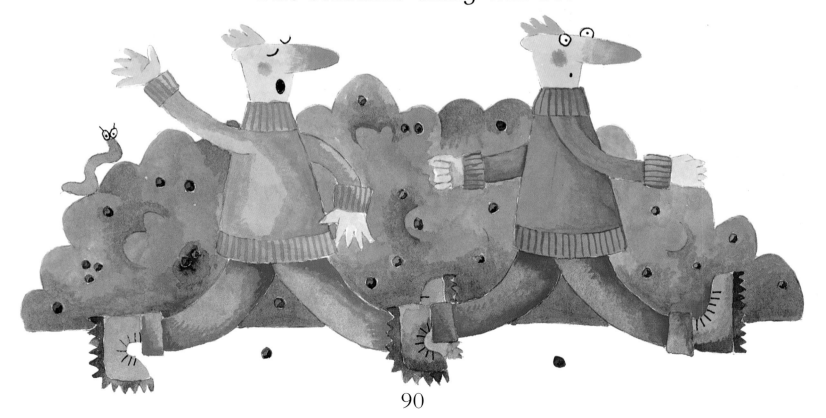

CROSS PATCH

Cross patch,
    Draw the latch,
Sit by the fire and spin;
    Take a cup,
    And drink it up,
Then call your neighbors in.

IT'S RAINING, IT'S POURING

It's raining, it's pouring,
The old man is snoring;
He went to bed and bumped his head
And couldn't get up in the morning.

THE MAIDEN FROM THE LAKE

There was once a shepherd who lived in Myddvai, by the mountains of Caermarthen. A great lake was near his pastures, and one day he was watching his sheep near its shores when he saw three beautiful maidens rise from the waters. The young women came to the shore, shook the water from their hair, and walked around among the sheep.

The shepherd was overcome by the beauty of the maiden who came nearest to him, and he offered her some bread from his pack. The girl took the bread, tried a little, and said to the shepherd, "Your bread's too hard. You won't catch me." Then she ran back to the lake with the others.

The shepherd wondered whether he would see the maidens again, but just in case, on the next day, he brought some bread that was not so well baked. To his delight, the maidens appeared again, and he offered the softer bread. But this time the girl said, "Your bread's not baked. You won't catch me." Once more, she returned to the water.

On the third day, the shepherd waited for the young woman. When she came, he offered her some bread that had been

floating on the water. This she liked, and the couple talked for a long while. Finally, the maiden agreed to marry the shepherd, but gave this warning: she would be a good wife to him, as good as any ordinary Welsh woman, unless he struck her three times without reason. The shepherd vowed that he would never do this, and the couple were soon married.

The shepherd and his bride were happy, and in time had three fine sons. It happened that they were going to christen one of the children when the wife said that it was too far to walk to church.

"Then go and get the horses," said the shepherd, "and we will ride all the way."

"While I get the horses, will you fetch my gloves from the house?" asked his wife.

But when the shepherd returned with the gloves he found that she had not fetched the horses, and he tapped her gently on the shoulder to remind her.

"That's one strike," said his wife.

A little while later, the pair were at a friend's wedding. The shepherd found his wife crying and again he tapped her on the shoulder as he asked her what was wrong.

"Trouble is coming for you," she replied. "That is the second time you have struck me without reason. Take care to avoid the third time."

From then on, the shepherd was careful not so much as to tap his wife, until one day the couple were at a funeral. All of a sudden, the wife began to laugh loudly. The shepherd was amazed. He could not understand why anyone should laugh at such a sad time, so, touching her rather roughly, he said, "Wife, why are you laughing when all around you are sad?"

"I am laughing because people who die leave their troubles behind them. But your troubles have just begun. You have struck me for a third time. Now I must make an end to our marriage and bid you farewell."

The shepherd knew that the time had come for his wife to leave him, and he was sad to the bottom of his heart. But he was still more surprised when he heard his wife calling all the cattle around her, bidding them follow her to her home

beneath the waters of the lake. He saw all his cattle, even a black calf that had recently been slaughtered and a team of oxen that were ploughing a field, get up and follow her away. The oxen even took their plough with them, cutting a deep furrow all the way to the shore.

The mark left by the plough can still be seen running across the pastures by the lake. But the lady has only been seen once more. When her sons had grown up, she returned to visit them. She gave them miraculous gifts of healing. And ever since, the Doctors of Myddvai have been famous throughout the land of Wales.

95

WHEN I WAS A BACHELOR

When I was a bachelor I lived by myself,
And all the meat I got I put upon a shelf;
The rats and the mice did lead me such a life
That I went to London to get myself a wife.

The streets were so broad and the lanes were
  so narrow,
I could not get my wife home without a
  wheelbarrow;
The wheelbarrow broke, my wife got a fall,
Down tumbled wheelbarrow, little wife, and all.

JACK SPRAT

Jack Sprat could eat no fat,
His wife could eat no lean,
And so between the two of them
They licked the platter clean.

OLD JOE BROWN

Old Joe Brown, he had a wife,
She was all of eight feet tall.
She slept with her head in the kitchen,
And her feet stuck out in the hall.

JEREMIAH

Jeremiah
Jumped in the fire.
Fire was so hot
He jumped in the pot.
Pot was so little
He jumped in the kettle.
Kettle was so black
He jumped in the crack.
Crack was so high
He jumped in the sky.
Sky was so blue
He jumped in a canoe.
Canoe was so deep
He jumped in the creek.
Creek was so shallow
He jumped in the tallow.
Tallow was so soft
He jumped in the loft.
Loft was so rotten
He jumped in the cotton.
Cotton was so white
He jumped all night.

99

OLD JOHN MUDDLECOMBE

Old John Muddlecombe lost his cap,
He couldn't find it anywhere, the poor old chap.
He walked down the High Street, and everybody said,
"Silly John Muddlecombe, you've got it on your head!"

POOR OLD ROBINSON CRUSOE

Poor old Robinson Crusoe!
Poor old Robinson Crusoe!
   They made him a coat
   Of an old nanny goat,

   I wonder how they could do so!
With a ring a ting tang,
And a ring a ting tang,
   Poor old Robinson Crusoe!

RUB-A-DUB DUB

Rub-a-dub dub,
Three men in a tub,
And who do you think they be?
The butcher, the baker,
The candlestick maker,
And they all jumped out of a rotten potato.

DOCTOR FOSTER WENT TO GLO'STER

Doctor Foster went to Glo'ster,
  In a shower of rain;
He stepped in a puddle, up to his middle,
  And never went there again.

PETER, PETER, PUMPKIN EATER

Peter, Peter, pumpkin eater,
Had a wife and couldn't keep her;
He put her in a pumpkin shell
And there he kept her very well.

Peter, Peter, pumpkin eater,
Had another and didn't love her;
Peter learned to read and spell,
And then he loved her very well.

SIMPLE SIMON

Simple Simon met a pieman
   Going to the fair;
Said Simple Simon to the pieman,
   "Let me taste your ware."

Said the pieman to Simple Simon,
   "Show me first your penny";
Said Simple Simon to the pieman,
   "Indeed I have not any."

UNCLE JOHN IS VERY SICK

Uncle John is very sick, what shall we send him?

A piece of pie, a piece of cake, a piece of apple dumpling.

What shall we send it in? In a piece of paper.

Paper is not fine enough; in a golden saucer.

Who shall we send it by? By the governor's daughter.

Take her by the lily-white hand, and lead her over the water.

AT THE SIEGE OF BELLE-ISLE

At the siege of Belle-isle
I was there all the while,
All the while, all the while,
At the siege of Belle-isle.

AUTUMN FIRES

In the other gardens
   And all up the vale,
From the autumn bonfires
   See the smoke trail!

Pleasant summer over
   And all the summer flowers,
The red fire blazes,
   The grey smoke towers.

Sing a song of seasons!
   Something bright in all!
Flowers in the summer,
   Fires in the fall!

ROBERT LOUIS STEVENSON

THE ENCHANTMENT
OF EARL GERALD

Earl Gerald was one of the bravest leaders in Ireland long ago. He lived in a castle at Mullaghmast with his lady and his knights, and whenever Ireland was attacked, Earl Gerald was among the first to join the fight to defend his homeland.

As well as being a great fighter, Gerald was also a magician who could change himself into any shape or form that he wanted. His wife was fascinated by this, but had never seen Gerald change his shape, although she had often asked him to show her how he could transform himself into the shape of some strange beast. Gerald always put her off with some excuse, until one day her pleading got too much for him.

"Very well," said Earl Gerald. "I will do what you ask. But you must promise not to show any fear when I change my shape. If you are frightened, I will not be able to change myself back again for hundreds of years."

She protested that the wife of such a noble warrior, who had seen him ride into battle against fearsome enemies, would not be frightened by such a small thing, so Gerald agreed to change his shape.

They were sitting quietly in the great chamber of the castle when suddenly Gerald vanished and a beautiful goldfinch was flying around the room. His wife was shocked by the sudden change, but did her best to stay calm and keep her side of the bargain. All went well, and she watched the little bird fly out into the garden, return, and perch in her lap. Gerald's wife was delighted with the bird, and smiled merrily, when suddenly and without warning, a great hawk swooped through the open windows, diving towards the finch. The lady screamed, even though the hawk missed Gerald and crashed into the table top, where its sharp beak stuck into the wood.

The damage was done. Gerald's wife had shown her fear. As she looked down to where the goldfinch had perched, she realised that the tiny bird had vanished. She never saw either the goldfinch or Earl Gerald again.

Many hundreds of years have passed by since Earl Gerald disappeared, and his poor wife is long dead. But occasionally, Gerald may be seen. Once in seven years, he mounts his steed and is seen riding around the Curragh of Kildare. Those few who have glimpsed him say that his horse has shoes made of silver, and the story goes that when these shoes are finally worn away, Gerald will return, fight a great battle, and rule as King of Ireland for forty years.

Meanwhile, in a great cavern beneath the old castle of Mullaghmast, Gerald and his knights sleep their long sleep. They are dressed in full armor and sit around a long table with the Earl at the head. Their horses, saddled and bridled, stand ready. When the right moment comes, a young lad with six fingers on each hand will blow a trumpet to awaken them.

Once, almost one hundred years ago, Earl Gerald was on one of his seven-yearly rides and an old horse dealer was passing the cavern where Gerald's knights were still sleeping. There were lights in the cavern, and the horse dealer went in to have a look. He was amazed to see the knights in their armor, all slumped on the table fast asleep, and the fine horses waiting there. He was looking at their steeds, and thinking whether he might lead one of the beasts away to market, when he dropped

the bridle he was holding. The clattering of the falling bridle echoed in the cavern and one of the knights stirred in his slumber.

"Has the time come?" groaned the knight, his voice husky with sleep. The horse dealer was struck dumb for a moment, as the knight's voice echoed in the cave. Finally he replied.

"No, the time has not come yet. But it soon will."

The knight slumped back on to the table, his helmet giving a heavy clank on the board. The horse dealer ran away home with all the speed he could manage. And Earl Gerald's knights slept on.

EVENING

(In words of one syllable)

The day is past, the sun is set,
   And the white stars are in the sky;
While the long grass with dew is wet,
   And through the air the bats now fly.

The lambs have now lain down to sleep,
   The birds have long since sought their nests;
The air is still, and dark, and deep
   On the hill side the old wood rests.

Yet of the dark I have no fear,
   But feel as safe as when 'tis light;
For I know God is with me there,
   And He will guard me through the night.

For God is by me when I pray,
   And when I close mine eyes in sleep,
I know that He will with me stay,
   And will all night watch by me keep.

For He who rules the stars and sea,
   Who makes the grass and trees to grow,
Will look on a poor child like me,
   When on my knees I to Him bow.

He holds all things in His right hand,
   The rich, the poor, the great, the small;
When we sleep, or sit, or stand,
   Is with us, for He loves us all.

THOMAS MILLER

THE SONG OF THE STARS

We are the stars which sing,
We sing with our light.
We are the birds of fire
We fly over the sky,
Our light is a voice.
We make a road for spirits,
For the spirits to pass over.

Among us are three hunters
Who chase a bear;
There never was a time
When they were not hunting.
We look down on the mountains.
This is the song of the stars.

ANONYMOUS
NATIVE AMERICAN, PASSAMAQUODDY

115

MINNIE AND WINNIE

Minnie and Winnie
  Slept in a shell.
Sleep, little ladies!
  And they slept well.

Pink was the shell within,
  Silver without;
Sounds of the great sea
  Wandered about.

Sleep, little ladies,
  Wake not soon!
Echo on echo
  Dies to the moon.

Two bright stars
    Peeped into the shell.
"What are they dreaming of?
    Who can tell?"

Started a green linnet
    Out of the croft;
Wake, little ladies,
    The sun is aloft!

ALFRED, LORD TENNYSON

MEG MERRILEES

Old Meg she was a Gipsy,
   And lived upon the moors:
Her bed it was the brown heath turf,
   And her house was out of doors.

Her apples were swart blackberries,
   Her currants pods o'broom;
Her wind was dew of the wild white rose,
   Her book a churchyard tomb.

Her Brothers were the craggy hills,
   Her Sisters larchen trees;
Alone with her great family
   She lived as she did please.

No breakfast had she many a morn,
   No dinner many a noon,
And 'stead of supper she would stare
   Full hard against the Moon.

But every morn of woodbine fresh
  She made her garlanding,
And every night the dark glen Yew
  She wove, and she would sing.

And with her fingers, old and brown,
  She plaited Mats o' Rushes,
And gave them to the Cottagers
  She met among the Bushes.

Old Meg was brave as Margaret Queen,
  And tall as Amazon;
An old red blanket cloak she wore;
  A chip hat had she on.
God rest her aged bones somewhere—
  She died full long agone!

JOHN KEATS

AIKEN DRUM

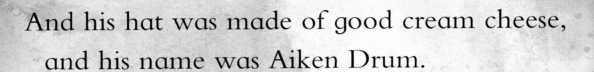

There was a man lived in the moon,
  and his name was Aiken Drum
And he played upon a ladle,
  and his name was Aiken Drum.

And his hat was made of good cream cheese,
  and his name was Aiken Drum.

And his coat was made of good roast beef,
  and his name was Aiken Drum.

And his buttons were made of penny loaves,
  and his name was Aiken Drum.

His waistcoat was made of crust of pies,
  and his name was Aiken Drum.

His breeches were made of haggis bags,
  and his name was Aiken Drum.
And he played upon a ladle,
  and his name was Aiken Drum.

120

There was a man in another town,
and his name was Willy Wood;
And he played upon a razor,
and his name was Willy Wood.

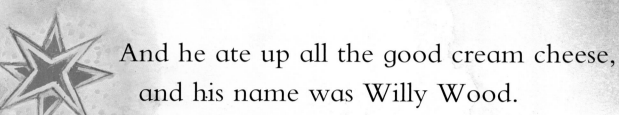

And he ate up all the good cream cheese,
and his name was Willy Wood.

And he ate up all the good roast beef,
and his name was Willy Wood.

And he ate up all the penny loaves,
and his name was Willy Wood.

And he ate up all the good pie crust,
and his name was Willy Wood.

But he choked upon the haggis bags,
and there was an end of Willy Wood.
And he played upon a razor,
and his name was Willy Wood.

ANONYMOUS
SCOTTISH

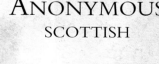

HERE COMES A WIDOW

Here comes a widow from Barbary-land,
With all her children in her hand;
One can brew, and one can bake,
And one can make a wedding cake.
  Pray take one,
  Pray take two,
Pray take one that pleases you.

MISS MARY MACK

Miss Mary Mack, Mack, Mack,
All dressed in black, black, black,
With silver buttons, buttons, buttons,
All down her back, back, back.
She went upstairs to make her bed,
She made a mistake and bumped her head;
She went downstairs to wash the dishes,
She made a mistake and washed her wishes;
She went outside to hang her clothes,
She made a mistake and hung her nose.

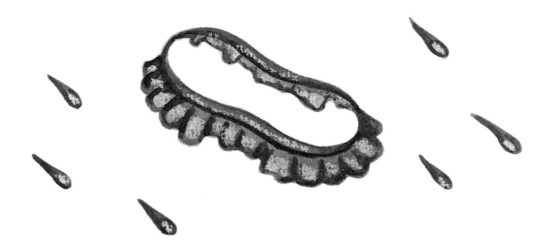

GILLY SILLY JARTER

Gilly Silly Jarter,
Who has lost a garter?
In a shower of rain,
The miller found it,
The miller ground it,
And the miller gave it to Silly again.

MR. PUNCHINELLO

Oh! mother, I shall be married to Mr. Punchinello.
    To Mr. Punch,
    To Mr. Joe,
    To Mr. Nell,
    To Mr. Lo,
    Mr. Punch, Mr. Joe,
    Mr. Nell, Mr. Lo,
    To Mr. Punchinello.

GOLDY LOCKS, GOLDY LOCKS

Goldy locks, goldy locks,
   Wilt thou be mine?
Thou shalt not wash dishes,
   Nor yet feed the swine;

But sit on a cushion,
   And sew a fine seam,
And feed upon strawberries,
   Sugar and cream.

LAVENDER'S BLUE

Lilies are white,
Rosemary's green;
When you are king,
I will be queen.

Roses are red,
Lavender's blue;
If you will have me,
I will have you.

THE FROG

A widow was baking in her kitchen and asked her daughter to go down to the well to fetch some water. Off the daughter went, down to the well by the meadow, but when she came to the well she found that it was dry. She wondered what she and her mother would do without water, for it was high summer and there had not been a cloud in the sky for days. And the poor girl was so anxious that she sat down beside the well and began to cry.

Suddenly, through her sobbing, the girl heard a plop, and a frog jumped out of the well.

"What are you crying for?" asked the frog.

The girl explained that there was no water and she did not know what to do.

"Well," said the frog, "if you will be my wife, you shall have all the water you need."

The girl thought that the creature was making fun of her, so she went along with the joke, and agreed to be the frog's wife. She lowered her bucket into the well once more, and sure enough, when she pulled it up, the bucket was full of water.

The girl took the water back to her mother, and thought no more about the frog until it was evening. Then, as the girl and her mother were about to go to bed, they heard a small voice and a scratching sound at the door of their cottage: "Open the door, my own true love. Remember the promise you made to me, when fetching your water down at the well."

"Ugh, it's a filthy frog," said the girl.

"Open the door to the poor creature," said her mother, for she was a gentle woman who liked to be kind to animals. And so they opened the door.

"Give me my supper, my own true love. Remember the promise you made to me, when fetching your water down at the well," the frog went on.

"Ugh, I don't want to feed the filthy beast," said the daughter.

"Give the poor creature something to eat," insisted her mother. So they laid out some food and the frog ate it all up thankfully.

"Put me to bed, my own true love. Remember the promise you made to me, when fetching your water down at the well," said the frog.

"Ugh, we can't have that slimy thing in our bed," protested the daughter.

"Put the poor creature to bed and let it rest," said the mother. So they turned down the sheets and the frog climbed into bed.

Then the frog spoke again: "Bring me an ax, my own true love. Remember the promise you made to me, when fetching your water down at the well."

The widow and her daughter looked at each other in deep puzzlement. "What would the creature want with an ax?" asked the girl. "It is far too heavy for a frog to lift."

"Fetch him an ax," said the mother. "We shall see soon

enough." So the daughter
went out to the woodshed
and returned with the ax.

"Now chop off my head,
my own true love. Remember
the promise you made to me,
when fetching your water
down at the well," croaked
the frog to the daughter.

Trembling, the girl turned to
the frog, who stretched out his
neck obligingly. She raised the
ax high, just as she did when
chopping wood for the fire, and brought it down on to the
frog's neck. When she had done the deed, the girl looked away
for a moment, scared to see the dead creature and its severed
head. But when she heard her mother's shout of surprise
she looked back quickly. And there stood the finest, most
handsome young prince that either of them had ever seen.

"It was me you promised to marry," smiled the prince.

And the poor widow's daughter and the handsome prince *did*
marry, and they lived in happiness for rest of their lives.

THE WISE OLD OWL

There was an old owl who lived in an oak;
The more he heard, the less he spoke.
The less he spoke, the more he heard.
Why aren't we like that wise old bird!

THERE WAS AN OLD CROW

There was an old crow
    Sat upon a clod:
There's an end of my song,
    That's odd!

FIRE ON THE MOUNTAIN

Rats in the garden—catch'em Towser!
Cows in the cornfield—run boys run!
Cat's in the cream pot—stop her now, sir!
Fire on the mountain—run boys run!

BILLY BOOSTER

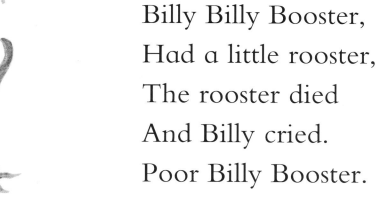

Billy Billy Booster,
Had a little rooster,
The rooster died
And Billy cried.
Poor Billy Booster.

MY SHADOW

I have a little shadow that goes in and out with me,
And what can be the use of him is more than I can see.
He is very, very like me from the heels up to the head;
And I see him jump before me,
  when I jump into my bed.

The funniest thing about him is the way he likes to grow—
Not at all like proper children, which is always very slow;
For he sometimes shoots up taller like an india rubber ball,
And he sometimes gets so little that
  there's none of him at all.

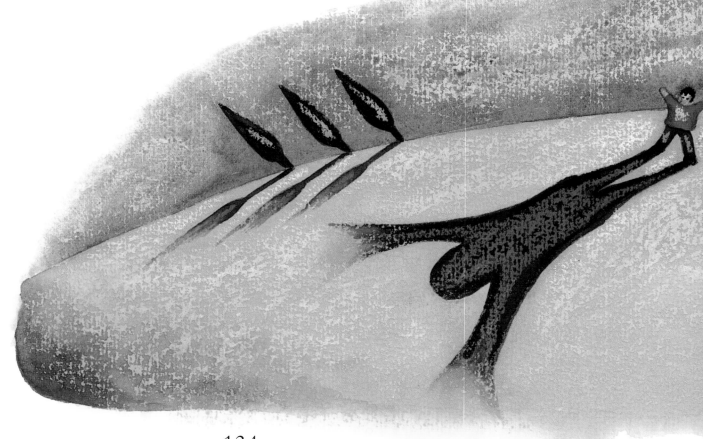

He hasn't got a notion of how children ought to play,
And can only make a fool of me in every sort of way.
He stays so close beside me, he's a coward you can see;
I'd think shame to stick to nursie
  as that shadow sticks to me!

One morning, very early, before the sun was up,
I rose and found the shining dew on every buttercup;
But my lazy little shadow, like an arrant sleepyhead,
Had stayed at home behind me and was
  fast asleep in bed.

ROBERT LOUIS STEVENSON

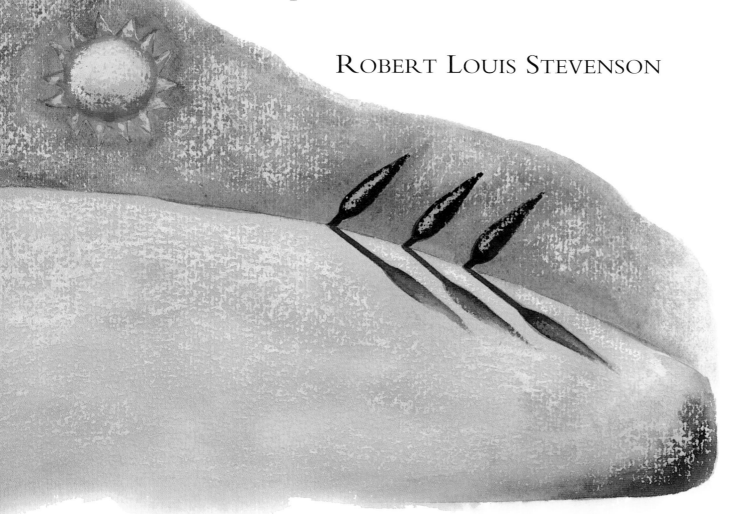

LIE A-BED

Lie a-bed,
Sleepy head,
Shut up eyes, bo-peep;
Till daybreak
Never wake:—
Baby, sleep.

CHRISTINA ROSSETTI

HAPPY THOUGHT

The world is so full of a number of things,
I'm sure we should all be as happy as kings.

ROBERT LOUIS STEVENSON

SKILLYWIDDEN

A man was cutting furze on Trendreen Hill one fine day, and he saw one of the little people stretched out, fast asleep, on the heath. The man took off the thick cuff that he wore at his work, crept up quietly, and popped the little man into the cuff before he could wake up. Then he carried his find home with care, and let the creature out on to the hearth stone.

When he awoke, the fairy looked quite at home and soon began to enjoy himself playing with the children. They called him Bob of the Heath, and Bob told the man that he would show him where to find crocks of gold hidden on the hillside.

Several days later, the neighbours joined together to bring away the harvest of furze, and all came to the man's house to celebrate the end of their task with a hearty meal. To hide Bob away from prying eyes, the man locked him in the barn with the children.

But the fairy and his playmates were cunning, and soon found a way out of the barn. Before long they were playing a game of dancing and hide-and-seek all around the great heap of furze in the yard.

As they played, they saw a tiny man and woman searching round the furze. "Oh my poor Skillywidden," said the tiny woman. "Where can you be? Will I ever set eyes on you again?"

"Go back indoors," said Bob to the children. "My mother and father have come looking for me. I must go back with them now." Then he cried, "Here I am mommy!" And before the children knew what had happened, their playmate Bob had vanished with his parents, and they were left in the yard.

When they told their father what had happened, the man was angry, and gave them a beating for escaping from the locked barn.

After this the furze-cutter sometimes went to Trendreen Hill to look for fairies and crocks of gold. But he was never able to find either.

A GOOD PLAY

We built a ship upon the stairs
All made of the back-bedroom chairs,
And filled it full of sofa pillows
To go a-sailing on the billows.

We took a saw and several nails,
And water in the nursery pails;
And Tom said, "Let us also take
An apple and a slice of cake";
Which was enough for Tom and me
To go a-sailing on, till tea.

We sailed along for days and days,
And had the very best of plays;
But Tom fell out and hurt his knee,
So there was no one left but me.

ROBERT LOUIS STEVENSON

THE LITTLE DOLL

I once had a sweet little doll, dears,
  The prettiest doll in the world;
Her cheeks were so red and so white, dears,
  And her hair was so charmingly curled.
But I lost my poor little doll, dears,
  As I played in the heath one day;
And I cried for her more than a week, dears;
  But I never could find where she lay.

I found my poor little doll, dears,
  As I played in the heath one day:
Folks say she is terribly changed, dears,
  For her paint is all washed away,
And her arm trodden off by the cows, dears
  And her hair not the least bit curled:
Yet for old sakes' sake she is still, dears,
  The prettiest doll in the world.

CHARLES KINGSLEY

BROTHER AND SISTER

"Sister, sister go to bed!
Go and rest your weary head."
Thus the prudent brother said.

"Do you want a battered hide,
Or scratches to your face applied?"
Thus his sister calm replied.

"Sister, do not raise my wrath.
I'd make you into mutton broth
As easily as kill a moth!"

The sister raised her beaming eye
And looked on him indignantly
And sternly answered, "Only try!"

Off to the cook he quickly ran.
"Dear Cook, please lend a frying-pan
To me as quickly as you can."

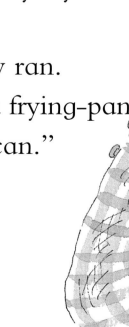

"And wherefore should I lend it you?"
"The reason, Cook, is plain to view.
I wish to make an Irish stew."
"What meat is in that stew to go?"
"My sister'll be the contents!"
                    "Oh!"
"You'll lend the pan to me, Cook?"
                    "No!"

Moral: Never stew your sister.

LEWIS CARROLL

143

OH FAIR TO SEE

Oh fair to see
Bloom-laden cherry tree,
   Arrayed in sunny white,
   An April day's delight;
Oh fair to see!

Oh fair to see
Fruit-laden cherry tree,
   With balls of shining red
   Decking a leafy head;
Oh fair to see!

CURRANTS ON A BUSH

Currants on a bush
   And figs upon a stem,
And cherries on a bending bough,
   And Ned to gather them.

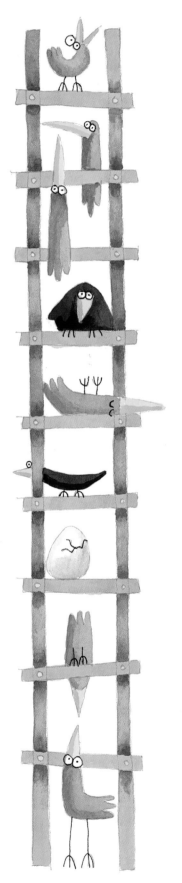

WHEN THE COW'S COME HOME

When the cows come home the milk is coming,
Honey's made while the bees are humming;
Duck and drake on the rushy lake,
And the deer live safe in the breezy brake;
And timid, funny, brisk little bunny
Winks his nose and sits all sunny.

WRENS AND ROBINS
IN THE HEDGE

Wrens and robins in the hedge,
  Wrens and robins here and there;
Building, perching, pecking, fluttering,
  Everywhere!

GOING DOWN HILL ON A BICYCLE

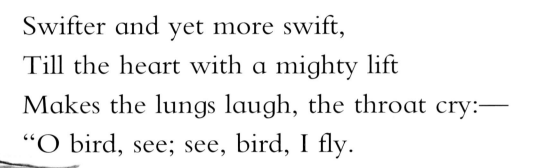

With lifted feet, hands still,
I am poised, and down the hill
Dart, with heedful mind;
The air goes by in a wind.

Swifter and yet more swift,
Till the heart with a mighty lift
Makes the lungs laugh, the throat cry:—
"O bird, see; see, bird, I fly.

"Is this, is this your joy?
O bird, then I, though a boy,
For a golden moment share
Your feathery life in air!"

Say, heart, is there aught like this
In a world that is full of bliss?
'Tis more than skating, bound
Steel-shod to the level ground.

Speed slackens now, I float
Awhile in my airy boat;
Till, when the wheels scarce crawl,
My feet to the treadles fall.

Alas, that the longest hill
Must end in a vale; but still,
Who climbs with toil, wheresoe'er,
Shall find wings waiting there.

HENRY CHARLES BEECHING

A CHILD'S LAUGHTER

All the bells of heaven may ring,
All the birds of heaven may sing,
All the wells on earth may spring,
All the winds on earth may bring
  All sweet sounds together;
Sweeter far than all things heard,
Hand of harper, tone of bird,
Sound of woods at sundawn stirred,
Welling water's winsome word,
  Wind in warm wan weather.

One thing yet there is, that none
Hearing ere its chime be done
Knows not well the sweetest one
Heard of man beneath the sun,
  Hoped in heaven hereafter;
Soft and strong and loud and light,
Very sound of very light
Heard from morning's rosiest height,
When the soul of all delight
  Fills a child's clear laughter.

Golden bells of welcome rolled
Never forth such notes, nor told
Hours so blithe in tones so bold,
As the radiant mouth of gold
    Here that rings forth heaven.
If the golden-crested wren
Were a nightingale—why, then,
Something seen and heard of men
Might be half as sweet as when
    Laughs a child of seven.

ALGERNON CHARLES SWINBURNE

I REMEMBER, I REMEMBER

I remember, I remember
The house where I was born,
The little window where the sun
Came peeping in at morn;
He never came a wink too soon
Nor brought too long a day;
But now, I often wish the night
Had borne my breath away.

I remember, I remember
The roses, red and white,
The violets, and the lily-cups—
Those flowers made of light!
The lilacs where the robin built,
And where my brother set
The laburnum on his birthday,—
The tree is living yet!

I remember, I remember
Where I was used to swing,
And thought the air must rush as fresh
To swallows on the wing;
My spirit flew in feathers then
That is so heavy now,
And summer pools could hardly cool
The fever on my brow.

I remember, I remember
The fir trees dark and high;
I used to think their slender tops
Were close against the sky:
It was a childish ignorance,
But now 'tis little joy
To know I'm farther off from Heaven
Than when I was a boy.

THOMAS HOOD

151

MEET-ON-THE-ROAD

"Now, pray, where are you going?"
  said Meet-on-the Road.
"To school, sir, to school sir,"
  said Child-as-it-Stood.

"What have you in your basket, child?"
  said Meet-on-the-Road.
"My dinner, sir, my dinner, sir,"
  said Child-as-it-Stood.

"What have you for dinner, child?"
  said Meet-on-the-Road.
"Some pudding, sir, some pudding, sir,"
  said Child-as-it-Stood.

"Oh, then I pray, give me a share,"
  said Meet-on-the-Road.
"I've little enough for myself, sir"
  said Child-as-it-Stood.

"What have you got that cloak on for?"
  said Meet-on-the-Road.
"To keep the wind and cold from me,"
  said Child-as-it-Stood.

"I wish the wind would blow through you,"
  said Meet-on-the Road.
"Oh, what a wish! What a wish!"
  said Child-as-it-Stood.

"Pray, what are those bells ringing for?"
  said Meet-on-the Road.
"To ring bad spirits home again,"
  said Child-as-it Stood.

"Oh, then I must be going, child!"
  said Meet-on-the-Road.
"So fare you well, so fare you well,"
  said Child-as-it-Stood.

ANONYMOUS
SCOTTISH

MAKING A WIFE

In the village of New Abbey lived a man called Alexander Harg, and he was newly married. His wife was a fine-looking young woman, and some people thought that if the fairies got hold of her, they would kidnap her, so great was her beauty.

A little while after his marriage, Alexander was out on the shore fishing with his net. Nearby were two old boats, left stranded on the rocks. He did not go too near for he had heard stories of little people being heard around them.

Sure enough, before long, Alexander heard a noise coming from one of the boats as if people were using hammers and chisels in there. Then a ghostly voice spoke up from the other old boat: "What are you doing in there?"

"Making a wife for Alexander Harg," came the reply.

Alexander, astounded and terrified by what he had heard, thought of nothing but running back home to see if his wife was safe. He burst through the door, locked it behind him, and took his young wife in his arms. Then he went round closing all the windows and making sure that no one could get in.

At midnight there came a loud banging at the door. The wife got up to open it. "Do not open the door," whispered Alexander. "There are strange things afoot this night."

So they sat together quietly, and after a while the knocking stopped. But just as they were relaxing again, the animals began to make terrifying bloodcurdling noises. The pair of them stayed indoors, and did not open the door until morning.

When they did so, they found a statue, carved in oak, in the shape and likeness of Alexander's wife. The good man made a bonfire and burned the effigy, and hoped never to hear the ghostly voices again.

THE KANGAROO

Old Jumpety-Bumpety-Hop-and-Go-One
Was lying asleep on his side in the sun.
This old kangaroo, he was whisking the flies
(With his long glossy tail) from his ears and his eyes.
Jumpety-Bumpety-Hop-and-Go-One
Was lying asleep on his side in the sun,
Jumpety-Bumpety-Hop!

ANONYMOUS
AUSTRALIAN

THE EAGLE

He clasps the crag with crooked hands;
Close to the sun in lonely lands,
Ring'd with the azure world, he stands.

The wrinkled sea beneath him crawls;
He watches from his mountain walls,
And like a thunderbolt he falls.

ALFRED, LORD TENNYSON

THE SNAKE

A narrow fellow in the grass
Occasionally rides;
You may have met him, —did you not?
His notice sudden is.

The grass divides as with a comb,
A spotted shaft is seen;
And then it closes at your feet
And opens further on.

He likes a boggy acre,
A floor too cool for corn.
Yet when a child, and barefoot,
I more than once, at morn,

Have passed, I thought, a whip-lash
Unbraiding in the sun,—
When, stooping to secure it,
It wrinkled, and was gone.

Several of nature's people
I know, and they know me;
I feel for them a transport
Of cordiality;

But never met this fellow,
Attended or alone,
Without a tighter breathing,
And zero at the bone.

EMILY DICKINSON

THE TYGER

Tyger! Tyger! burning bright
In the forests of the night,
What immortal hand or eye
Could frame thy fearful symmetry?

In what distant deeps or skies
Burnt the fire of thine eyes?
On what wings dare he aspire?
What the hand dare seize the fire?

And what shoulder, and what art,
Could twist the sinews of thy heart?
And, when thy heart began to beat,
What dread hand? and what dread feet?

What the hammer? what the chain?
In what furnace was thy brain?
What the anvil, what dread grasp
Dare its deadly terrors clasp?

When the stars threw down their spears,
And water'd heaven with their tears,
Did he smile his work to see?
Did he who made the Lamb make thee?

Tyger! Tyger! burning bright
In the forests of the night,
What immortal hand or eye,
Dare frame thy fearful symmetry?

WILLIAM BLAKE

THE CAMEL'S COMPLAINT

Canary-birds feed on sugar and seed,
  Parrots have crackers to crunch;
And as for the poodles, they tell me the noodles
  Have chicken and cream for their lunch.
    But there's never a question
    About *my* digestion—
      Anything does for me.

Cats, you're aware, can repose in a chair,
  Chickens can roost upon rails;
Puppies are able to sleep in a stable,
  And oysters can slumber in pails.
    But no one supposes
    A poor camel dozes—
      Any place does for me.

Lambs are enclosed where it's never exposed,
  Coops are constructed for hens;
Kittens are treated to houses well heated,
  And pigs are protected by pens.
    But a camel comes handy
    Wherever it's sandy—
      Anywhere does for me.

People would laugh if you rode a giraffe,
  Or mounted the back of an ox;
It's nobody's habit to ride on a rabbit,
  Or try to bestraddle a fox.
    But as for a camel, he's
    Ridden by families—
      Any load does for me.

A snake is as round as a hole in the ground,
  And weasels are wavy and sleek;
And no alligator could ever be straighter
  Than lizards that live in a creek.
    But a camel's all lumpy
    And bumpy and humpy—
      Any shape does for me.

CHARLES F. CARRYL

MOTHER TABBYSKINS

Sitting at a window
In her cloak and hat
I saw Mother Tabbyskins,
The *real* old cat!
  Very old, very old,
   Crumplety and lame;
Teaching kittens how to scold—
   Is it not a shame?

Kittens in the garden
Looking in her face,
Learning how to spit and swear—
  Oh, what a disgrace!
  Very wrong, very wrong,
   Very wrong and bad;
Such a subject for our song,
   Makes us all too sad.

Old Mother Tabbyskins,
Sticking out her head,
Gave a howl, and then a yowl,
  Hobbled off to bed.

Very sick, very sick,
Very savage, too;
Pray send for a doctor quick—
Any one will do!

Doctor Mouse came creeping,
Creeping to her bed;
Lanced her gums and felt her pulse,
Whispered she was dead.
Very sly, very sly,
The *real* old cat
Open kept her weather eye—
Mouse! beware of that!

Old Mother Tabbyskins,
Saying "Serves him right",
Gobbled up the doctor, with
Infinite delight.
Very fast, very fast,
Very pleasant, too—
"What a pity it can't last!
Bring another, do!"

ELIZABETH ANNA HART

TWO LITTLE KITTENS

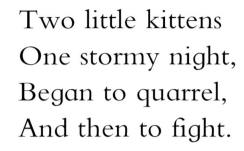

Two little kittens
One stormy night,
Began to quarrel,
And then to fight.

One had a mouse
And the other had none;
And that was the way
The quarrel begun.

"I'll have that mouse,"
Said the bigger cat.
"You'll have that mouse?
We'll see about that!"

"I will have that mouse,"
Said the tortoise-shell;
And, spitting and scratching,
On her sister she fell.

I've told you before
'Twas a stormy night,
When these two kittens
Began to fight.

A hundred pounds will set you free,
My fair lady.

We have not a hundred pounds,
Pounds, pounds, pounds; pounds, pounds, pounds;
We have not a hundred pounds,
My fair lady.

Then to prison you must go,
Go, go, go; go, go, go;
Then to prison you must go,
My fair lady.

To prison we will not go,
Go, go, go; go, go, go;
To prison we will not go,
My fair lady.

ALONE

From childhood's hour I have not been
As others were,—I have not seen
As others saw,—I could not bring
My passions from a common spring.
From the same source I have not taken
My sorrow; I could not awaken
My heart to joy at the same tone;
And all I loved, I loved alone.
Then—in my childhood—in the dawn
Of a most stormy life was drawn
From every depth of good and ill
The mystery which binds me still:
From the torrent, or the fountain,
From the red cliff of the mountain,
From the sun that round me rolled
In its autumn tint of gold,—
From the lightning in the sky
As it passed me flying by,—
From the thunder and the storm,
And the cloud that took the form
(When the rest of Heaven was blue)
Of a demon in my view.

EDGAR ALLAN POE

170

ABOU BEN ADHEM

Abou Ben Adhem (may his tribe increase!)
Awoke one night from a deep dream of peace,
And saw, within the moonlight in his room,
Making it rich, and like a lily in bloom,
An angel writing in a book of gold:—
Exceeding peace had made Ben Adhem bold,
And to the presence in the room he said,
"What writest thou?"—The vision raided its head,
And with a look made of all sweet accord,
Answered, "The names of those who love the Lord."
"And is mine one?" said Abou. "Nay, not so,"
Replied the angel. Abou spoke more low,
But cheerily still; and said, "I pray thee then,
Write me as one that loves his fellow-men."

The angel wrote, and vanished. The next night
It came again with a great wakening light,
And showed the names whom love of God had blessed,
And lo! Ben Adhem's name led all the rest.

LEIGH HUNT

THE BELLS OF LONDON

Gay go up and gay go down,
To ring the bells of London town.

Halfpence and farthings,
Say the bells of St. Martin's.

Oranges and lemons,
Say the bells of St. Clement's.

Pancakes and fritters,
Say the bells of St. Peter's.

Two sticks and an apple,
Say the bells of Whitechapel.

Kettles and pans,
Say the bells of St. Ann's.

You owe me ten shillings,
Say the bells of St. Helen's.

When will you pay me?
Say the bells of Old Bailey.

When I grow rich,
Say the bells of Shoreditch.

Pray when will that be?
Say the bells of Stepney.

I am sure I don't know,
Says the great bell of Bow.

AGAINST QUARRELING AND FIGHTING

Let dogs delight to bark and bite,
   For God hath made them so:
Let bears and lions growl and fight,
   For 'tis their nature, too.

But, children, you should never let
   Such angry passions rise:

Your little hands were never made
   To tear each other's eyes.

Let love through all your actions run,
   And all your words be mild:
Live like the blessed Virgin's Son,
   That sweet and lovely child.

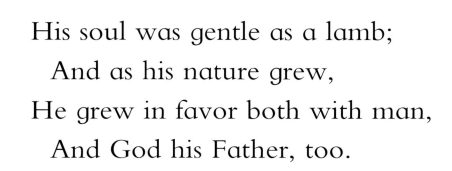

His soul was gentle as a lamb;
   And as his nature grew,
He grew in favor both with man,
   And God his Father, too.

Now, Lord of all, he reigns above,
   And from his heavenly throne
He sees what children dwell in love,
   And marks them for his own.

ISAAC WATTS

SNOW

In the gloom of whiteness,
In the great silence of snow,
A child was sighing
And bitterly saying: "Oh,
They have killed a white bird up there on her nest,
The down is fluttering from her breast!"
And still it fell through that dusky brightness
On the child crying for the bird of the snow.

EDWARD THOMAS

WINTER

When icicles hang by the wall,
   And Dick the shepherd blows his nail,
And Tom bears logs into the hall,
   And milk comes frozen home in pail;
When blood is nipp'd and ways be foul,
Then nightly sings the staring owl,
    To-whit! to-who!
    A merry note,
While greasy Joan doth keel the pot.

When all aloud the wind doth blow,
   And coughing drowns the parson's saw;
And birds sit brooding in the snow,
   And Marian's nose looks red and raw;
When roasted crabs hiss in the bowl,
Then nightly sings the staring owl,
    To-whit! to-who!
    A merry note,
While greasy Joan doth keel the pot.

WILLIAM SHAKESPEARE

THE SUGAR-PLUM TREE

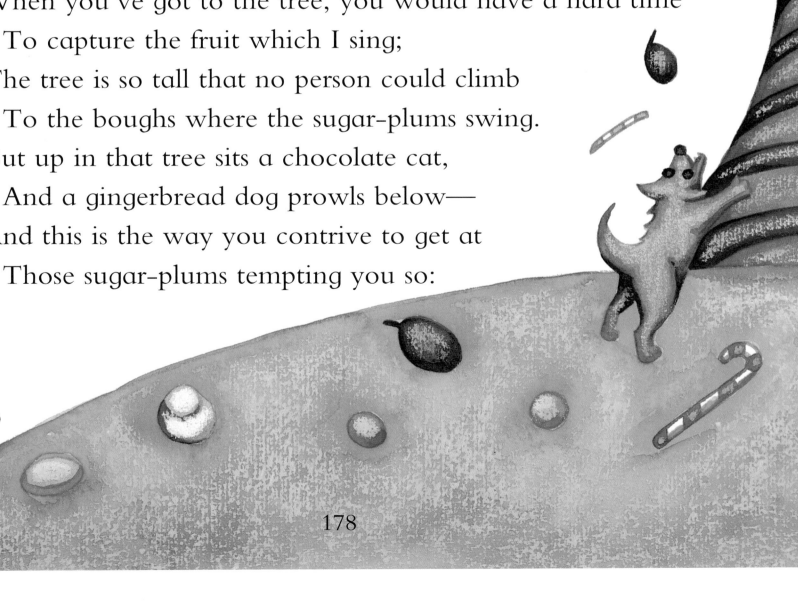

Have you ever heard of the Sugar-Plum Tree?
　'Tis a marvel of great renown!
It blooms on the shore of the Lollipop sea
　In the garden of Shut-Eye Town:
The fruit that it bears is so wondrously sweet
　(As those who have tasted it say)
That good little children have only to eat
　Of that fruit to be happy next day.

When you've got to the tree, you would have a hard time
　To capture the fruit which I sing;
The tree is so tall that no person could climb
　To the boughs where the sugar-plums swing.
But up in that tree sits a chocolate cat,
　And a gingerbread dog prowls below—
And this is the way you contrive to get at
　Those sugar-plums tempting you so:

You say but the word to that gingerbread dog
   And he barks with such terrible zest
That the chocolate cat is at once all agog,
   As her swelling proportions attest.
And the chocolate cat goes cavorting around
   From this leafy limb unto that,
And the sugar-plums tumble, of course, to the ground—
   Hurrah for that chocolate cat!

There are marshmallows, gumdrops, and peppermint canes,
   With striplings of scarlet or gold,
And you carry away of the treasure that rains
   As much as your apron can hold!
So come, little child, cuddle closer to me
   In your dainty white nightcap and gown,
And I'll rock you away to that Sugar-Plum Tree
   In the garden of Shut-Eye Town.

EUGENE FIELD

LITTLE JACK HORNER

Little Jack Horner
Sat in a corner,
Eating his Christmas pie;
He put in his thumb,
And pulled out a plum,
And said: "What a good boy am I!"

WHEN JACKY'S A VERY GOOD BOY

When Jacky's a very good boy,
  He shall have cakes and a custard;
But when he does nothing but cry,
  He shall have nothing but mustard

LITTLE TOMMY TUCKER

Little Tommy Tucker
    Sings for his supper:
What shall we give him?
    Brown bread and butter.
How shall he cut it
    Without a knife?
How can he marry
    Without a wife?

NOW THRICE WELCOME CHRISTMAS

Now thrice welcome, Christmas,
  Which brings us good cheer,
Minc'd pies and plum porridge,
  Good ale and strong beer;
With pig, goose, and capon,
  The best that can be,
So well doth the weather
  And our stomachs agree.

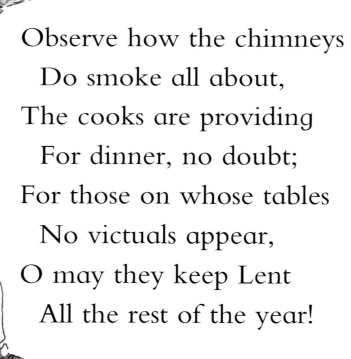

Observe how the chimneys
  Do smoke all about,
The cooks are providing
  For dinner, no doubt;
For those on whose tables
  No victuals appear,
O may they keep Lent
  All the rest of the year!

With holly and ivy
 So green and so gay,
We deck up our houses
 As fresh as the day,
With bays and rosemary,
 And laurel complete;
And every one now
 Is a king in conceit.

ANONYMOUS
ENGLISH

THE LAMB

Little lamb, who made thee?
  Dost thou know who made thee?
Gave thee life, and bid thee feed
By the stream and o'er the mead;
Gave thee clothing of delight,
Softest clothing, woolly, bright;
Gave thee such a tender voice,
Making all the vales rejoice?
  Little lamb, who made thee?
  Dost thou know who made thee?

Little lamb, I'll tell thee,
Little lamb, I'll tell thee:
He is callèd by thy name,
For he calls himself a lamb.
He is meek, and he is mild;
He became a little child.
I a child, and thou a lamb,
We are callèd by his name.
Little lamb, God bless thee!
Little lamb, God bless thee!

WILLIAM BLAKE

THE OXEN

Christmas Eve, and twelve of the clock.
  "Now they are all on their knees,"
An elder said as we sat in a flock
  By the embers in hearthside ease.

We pictured the meek mild creatures where
  They dwelt in their strawy pen,
Nor did it occur to one of us there
  To doubt they were kneeling then.

So fair a fancy few would weave
    In these years! Yet, I feel,
If someone said on Christmas Eve,
    "Come; see the oxen kneel

"In the lonely barton by yonder coomb
    Our childhood used to know,"
I should go with him in the gloom,
    Hoping it might be so.

THOMAS HARDY

CHRISTMAS BELLS

I heard the bells on Christmas Day
Their old familiar carols play,
  And wild and sweet
  The words repeat
Of Peace on earth, Goodwill to men!

And thought how, as the day had come,
The belfries of all Christendom
  Had rolled along
  The unbroken song
Of Peace on earth, Goodwill to men!

Till ringing, singing on its way,
The world revolved from night to day,
  A voice, a chime,
  A chant sublime,
Of Peace on earth, Goodwill to men!

Then from each black accursed mouth,
The cannon thundered in the South,
  And with the sound
  The carols drowned,
The Peace on earth, Goodwill to men!

And in despair I bowed my head;
"There is no peace on earth," I said,
  "For hate is strong
  And mocks the song
Of Peace on earth, Goodwill to men!"

Then peeled the bells more loud and deep:
"God is not dead, nor doth he sleep!
  The Wrong shall fail,
  The Right prevail,
With Peace on earth, Goodwill to men!"

HENRY WADSWORTH LONGFELLOW

IN THE TREE-TOP

"Rock-a-by, baby, up in the tree-top!"
 Mother his blanket is spinning;
And a light little rustle that never will stop,
 Breezes and boughs are beginning.
Rock-a-by, baby, swinging so high!
  Rock-a-by!

"When the wind blows, then the cradle will rock."
 Hush! now it stirs in the bushes;
Now with a whisper, a flutter of talk,
 Baby and hammock it pushes.
Rock-a-by, baby! shut, pretty eye!
  Rock-a-by!

"Rock with the boughs, rock-a-by, baby dear!"
 Leaf-tongues are singing and saying;
Mother she listens, and sister is near,
 Under the tree softly playing.
Rock-a-by, baby! mother's close by!
  Rock-a-by!

Weave him a beautiful dream, little breeze!
Little leaves, nestle around him!
He will remember the song of the trees,
When age with silver has crowned him.
Rock-a-by, baby! wake by-and-by!
Rock-a-by!

LUCY LARCOM

THE CAT OF CATS

I am the cat of cats. I am
    The everlasting cat!
Cunning, and old, and sleek as jam,
    The everlasting cat!
I hunt the vermin in the night—
    The everlasting cat!
For I see best without the light—
    The everlasting cat!

WILLIAM BRIGHTY RANDS